THE CRYSTAL ROSE

READ ALL OF THE
ENCHANTING ADVENTURES!

SNOW SISTERS

THE CRYSTAL ROSE

By **Astrid Foss**

Illustrated by **Monique Dong**

ALADDIN

NEW YORK LONDON TORONTO SYDNEY NEW DELHI

ALADDIN

An imprint of Simon & Schuster Children's Publishing Division
1230 Avenue of the Americas, New York, New York 10020
First Aladdin paperback edition December 2020
Text copyright © 2018 by Working Partners Ltd
Cover illustrations copyright © 2020 by Sharon Tancredi
Interior illustrations copyright © 2018 by Monique Dong
Originally published in Great Britain in 2018 by Nosy Crow Ltd
Also available in an Aladdin hardcover edition.

All rights reserved, including the right of reproduction in whole or in part in any form.
ALADDIN and related logo are registered trademarks of Simon & Schuster, Inc.
For information about special discounts for bulk purchases, please contact Simon & Schuster
Special Sales at 1-866-506-1949 or business@simonandschuster.com.
The Simon & Schuster Speakers Bureau can bring authors to your live event.
For more information or to book an event contact the Simon & Schuster Speakers Bureau
at 1-866-248-3049 or visit our website at www.simonspeakers.com.
Cover designed by Heather Palisi
The text of this book was set in GaramondDTInfant
Manufactured in the United States of America 0622 OFF
2 4 6 8 10 9 7 5 3
Library of Congress Cataloging-in-Publication Data
Names: Foss, Astrid, author. | Dong, Monique, illustrator.
Title: The crystal rose / by Astrid Foss ; illustrated by Monique Dong.
Description: First Aladdin hardcover edition. | New York : Aladdin Books, 2020. | Series: Snow
sisters ; 2 | Originally published in Great Britain by Nosy Crow Ltd. | Audience: Ages 7-10. |
Summary: Three princesses with magical powers face an icy journey to find the blue Everchanging
Light and the enchanted crystal rose in order to save their kingdom from the Shadow Witch.
Identifiers: LCCN 2020019054 (print) | LCCN 2020019055 (ebook) | ISBN 9781534443518
(paperback) | ISBN 9781534443525 (hardcover) | ISBN 9781534443532 (ebook)
Subjects: CYAC: Sisters—Fiction. | Triplets—Fiction. | Magic—Fiction. |
Adventure and adventurers—Fiction.
Classification: LCC PZ7.1.F672 Cr 2020 (print) | LCC PZ7.1.F672 (ebook) | DDC [Fic]—dc23
LC record available at https://lccn.loc.gov/2020019054
LC ebook record available at https://lccn.loc.gov/2020019055

Prologue

As the sun rose over the beautiful island of Nordovia, its golden rays lit up the icy mountain peaks, making them glitter and shine. Arctic hares hopped across the lowland plains, while polar bears emerged from their dens and rolled happily in the thick snow. In the villages, people were waking up, pulling on warm clothes, and getting ready to start their day. Everything seemed normal. But something was wrong.

Very wrong.

The magical lights that usually swirled across the skies in Nordovia—the Everchanging Lights that kept everything in balance and made the island such a wonderful place to live—had dimmed from their usual bright pink, purple, and blue to occasional pale flickers of color.

In the north of the land, in a freezing ice cave carved into the side of a jagged mountain by dark magic, a flame-haired woman looked out of the icy bars of her prison. Her face was etched with worry as she turned to her husband. "Oh, Magnus. Do you think our girls will be able to find the orbs and restore the Lights?"

He squeezed her shoulder. "We must have faith, Freya. If anyone can defeat the Shadow Witch, it is our daughters." He kissed her forehead. "They have their mother's determination—they will never give up."

She shot him a weak smile. "They have their father's courage, too. But their magical powers have only just awakened. It could take them many months to learn how to control them. My sister grows stronger by the day. She longs for power and if she finds the orbs first—" She broke off with a cry and doubled over.

"What is it, Freya?" asked Magnus, grabbing her hand.

"She . . . she is using spells to try to take my magic. I can feel it!" Freya gasped. Her face creased up in pain.

"Keep fighting her, my love," Magnus begged. "We must give our girls time to restore the Everchanging Lights to the island."

A triumphant laugh echoed through their prison. "Give in, Sister!" a voice hissed through the air. "You will never manage to keep your powers from me. I will take them."

"No!" Freya forced herself upright, her emerald eyes flashing. "I will not let you, Veronika. You must not be allowed to harm Nordovia!"

"You have no choice in the matter," snapped the voice of her sister, the Shadow Witch. Her form gradually emerged from a dark corner, and she strode over to a smooth sheet of ice on the floor. She closed her eyes and began to chant strange words. Images appeared on the surface of the ice.

Veronika cackled. "My magic allows me to spy on your darling daughters." She paused, glaring at Freya. "And I will destroy them without ever having to leave your side, *dear Sister*! Nobody is going to stop me. Soon the magic of

the Everchanging Lights will belong to me!"
Her laugh rang out, rising in volume, echoing
around and around the icy prison. Then she
trained the full force of her powerful magic
upon her sister.

Freya, with a scream of pain, crumpled to the floor.

Chapter One

Hanna Aurora gazed into the snow globe that stood on a table in the center of her and her sisters' bedchamber. Her emerald-green eyes were reflected back at her from its glass. *Start to glow, oh, please start to glow,* she thought longingly.

Inside the globe, soft white snowflakes swirled around a crystal-clear waterfall that fell endlessly into an icy sea. Pink light flickered softly through the snowflakes, lighting the globe. It was beautiful. Hanna and her sisters,

Ida and Magda, had always loved the snow globe, but it had become even more precious to them since their parents had been trapped by the Shadow Witch. Now it was the only way their mother could talk to them. Twice since she had been imprisoned, her image had appeared in the globe and twice she had given the girls advice. But her magic was fading fast.

Hanna itched with impatience. She wanted their mother to speak to them again. So much had happened in the last few days! The girls' evil aunt was desperate to steal the power of the Everchanging Lights. But their mother had used magic to contain the Lights inside three glass orbs—one pink, one blue, and one purple—and hidden them around the island to protect them from the Shadow Witch. The girls had already found the pink orb despite their aunt's attempts to stop them. If they could only find the blue and purple orbs too, they would be able to rescue their parents and restore peace to Nordovia.

Hanna gazed at the snow globe and remembered all that had happened. Just five days ago, she and her sisters had journeyed into the forest to find the pink orb. A giant wolf, sent by the Shadow Witch, had attacked them, but they had fought it off and brought the orb safely home. It had been an amazing adventure! The orb containing the pink Everchanging Light had been placed inside the snow globe to keep it safe.

We will get the blue and purple orbs, vowed Hanna, her mouth setting in a determined line. *We will free the Lights and rescue Mother and Father.*

She jumped to her feet. "Oh, I can't stand this any longer!" She pushed her hands through her choppy red hair. "We've got to do something.

We can't just sit around waiting for Mother to talk to us."

Her sisters looked up. Ida was sitting on her bed, sketching as usual, while Magda was stroking Oskar, their pet polar bear cub, who was snoozing on the floor next to her. Although the girls were triplets, they were very different! Ida was thoughtful and a little shy, and loved nothing more than painting or sketching. Magda was a good problem-solver and adored animals of all shapes and sizes, from the smallest butterfly to the largest polar bear. And Hanna was always on the move—keen to try something new and have an adventure! She found all of this waiting very difficult.

"Hanna, we've talked about this," said Ida, pushing her blond braid back over her shoulder. The triplets had the same green eyes but their hair was different—Hanna's was the deep red

of autumn leaves, Ida's was honey blond and Magda's was the dark brown of chocolate. "We have to wait until Mother finds a way to contact us again, otherwise we won't know where to look for the other orbs. We can't just rush off without knowing where we have to go."

"Why not?" demanded Hanna.

"Because it's not *sensible*," said Ida.

"So? It would be better than sitting around here having lessons with Madame Olga. We should be trying to save Nordovia!"

"We need guidance," Ida said. "A clue at least."

"Ida's right, Hanna," Magda put in. "We can't do anything until we get another message from Mother."

Hanna stamped her foot in frustration. "I can't believe you two! It's going to be the Day of the Midnight Sun in less than two weeks' time." She paced around the chamber. "If we don't find the remaining orbs by then, Aunt Veronika's powers will be strong enough to summon them to her. And then she'll rule Nordovia, and destroy everything! And what about Mother and Father? Don't you *want* to rescue them?"

"Of course we do!" said Ida. "I want to stop Aunt Veronika just as much as you do!"

"It doesn't seem like it!" huffed Hanna.

"Please don't fight," pleaded Magda. "Look . . ." Her gaze darted around the chamber as she searched for a way to calm the argument between her sisters. "We know we're going to have to go on another adventure soon to find the next orb. Why don't I use my magic to sneak into the kitchen and find some food we can take with us?"

Hanna nodded eagerly. "Oh yes! Use your magic!"

On their twelfth birthday, just a few days

ago, they had each developed magical powers. Members of the Aurora family, who were the Keepers of the Everchanging Lights, all discovered their unique magical powers on their twelfth birthday. Hanna had discovered she could move things using her mind, Ida had the power to bring objects to life when she drew them, and Magda could transform into any animal or bird that she saw. The triplets' mother, Freya, had the power to stop time and their aunt, Veronika, had the power to make plants and trees grow. Like all Auroras, both their mother and aunt had gradually learned other powers over the years. Freya had always used magic for good, but Veronika had learned dark magic. Her pursuit of power had turned her into the evil Shadow Witch—an enemy of Nordovia, the very land she was supposed to protect.

"What sort of animal will you turn into?" Ida asked Magda.

Magda tucked her brown hair behind her ears and smiled. "A mouse!"

Magda needed to see an animal in order to be able to turn into it, and so she went to the table beside her bed where she kept a tin of breadcrumbs. There was a little mouse secretly living in their bedchamber. Magda had found him in the courtyard one day. She had made him a home behind a loose bit of skirting board and fed him scraps of bread and cheese. He seemed to like his new home! Now Magda crouched down at the hole in the skirting board and put a few breadcrumbs on the wooden floor. "Erik!" she called.

A few seconds later, a little nose with trembling whiskers poked out. Smelling the food and seeing Magda, Erik the mouse scampered out of his hole and ran to the crumbs. He picked them up with his front paws and munched them quickly, looking at her with his little bright eyes.

Magda concentrated hard on him, imagining what it must feel like to be a mouse, to have a long tail and twitching whiskers. Her body started to tingle all over and she felt herself start to shrink. She blinked. Everything in the room was massive and instead of hands she had little tiny paws.

Hanna and Ida bent down and peered at her. "Magda?" Ida said.

Magda gave a squeak. Her sisters looked like

giants! Erik the mouse squeaked at her in surprise and ran back into his home in the skirting board. Magda made what she hoped was a thank-you squeak to him, then scampered across the floor and out through the gap underneath the bedchamber door. She hoped she wouldn't meet one of the castle cats. *I'll have to change back quickly if I do!* she realized.

She scurried down the stairs and along the passageway that led to the vast kitchen with its big iron ovens and stores of food.

She slipped under the door. It was warm inside. The cook—a large round lady with a big white apron—was bustling around, calling out instructions to the other servants, who were chopping vegetables and kneading dough. Two chambermaids were at the big wooden table darning socks, and the kitchen boy was stoking the fire in the oven.

Magda crept around the side of the room, staying in the shadows. She wanted to sneak into the pantry without anyone seeing her.

"I heard the master and mistress had been taken to a tower near Skordsberg," she heard one of the chambermaids saying.

Magda stiffened and paused. Was that true? Had the palace servants heard some news about her parents?

"No, that's not right," said the other maid,

shaking her head. "They're trapped under the Glittering Mountains in the east."

"The peddler told me that they're trapped in the heart of the Red Volcano," the kitchen boy put in.

Magda realized all she was hearing was gossip. She let out a sigh of frustration but it came out as a squeak.

The cook looked around sharply at the sound. "Mouse!" she exclaimed. She grabbed a broom and swept it angrily at Magda. "Oh no! Not in my kitchen, mouse. I'll get you!"

Magda dodged the broom just in time and turned and ran. So much for making it to the pantry! The chambermaids screamed and jumped onto their chairs. The broom slammed down behind Magda again, narrowly missing her tail. Magda squeaked in alarm and dived under the kitchen door, racing toward the staircase.

Madame Olga, the girls' governess, was proceeding up the stairs at a stately pace. *Help!* thought Magda. She had to get back to the chamber before Madame Olga did. Her strict governess would definitely not think that searching for food disguised as a mouse was suitable behavior for a young lady!

She leaped onto the wooden base of the bannister and scurried up the staircase, out of sight of Madame Olga. Then she tore along the corridor and darted under the door of the bedchamber. Magda willed herself to turn back to normal. A tingle ran down her spine and, in an instant, she was a girl again.

Her sisters rushed over.

"Are you all right?" Ida demanded, looking at her flushed face.

Magda nodded, gasping for breath and trying to calm her pounding heart.

"What happened?" asked Hanna.

"The cook saw me and tried to hit me with a broom!" Magda said, panting. "I didn't even get into the pantry to see what food there is." She remembered what else she had seen. "Oh yes, and I passed Madame Olga on the stairs—she's on her way up here!" She looked around and saw a pile of ice picks by the door and

noticed that the wardrobe had moved across
the room. "What's been happening here?"

Hanna grinned. "You're not the only one
who's been practicing magic!"

Just then the door opened and Madame
Olga swept in, her brown dress immaculate,
her hair tied back in a neat roll at the back of
her neck. "Ah, you're here, girls. I've been . . ."
She gave a gasp of surprise as she tripped over

the ice picks. "Oh my goodness! Whatever are all these doing here?"

"Sorry, Madame Olga!" said Ida. "I was practicing my drawing magic."

"Well, don't leave things lying around; put them in the bottom of the wardrobe for now and then take them outside later." Madame Olga turned to gesture to where the wardrobe usually was and blinked. "The wardrobe. It's gone!" she said faintly.

"It's, um . . . over there, Madame," said Hanna, grinning guiltily as she pointed to the wardrobe in its new place. "Sorry!"

Madame Olga put her hands on her hips. "Honestly, girls. Moving furniture, creating trip hazards. How am I ever going to turn you into young ladies?" She fixed Magda with a look. "And what have you been doing while your sisters have been creating havoc?"

"Me? Um . . . Just nature studies," said Magda, trying not to giggle.

"Hmm." Madame Olga didn't look convinced by her reply. "Well, I think you should all make yourselves useful. Please go into the garden and gather some flowers so that we can discuss their properties in tomorrow's nature lesson."

She swept back out, shutting the door sharply.

The girls looked at one another, waited until Madame Olga was safely out of earshot, and then burst out laughing. "Oh dear. Poor Madame Olga!" said Magda.

"Let's go into the garden to get some flowers and herbs," said Ida. "Oskar could do with a walk."

Oskar opened his eyes at the word *walk* and got to his feet. He was a roly-poly cub with the softest white fur and eyes the color of dark chocolate. He bounced over to the door and looked at the girls hopefully.

The sisters set off down the stairs with the little polar bear bounding at their heels. But before Ida could reach the garden, she realized she had left her beloved sketchbook in the room. She rushed back for it.

As Ida entered the room her eyes were caught by a soft glow coming from the snow globe. She stared. The glow got brighter, and the snow inside the globe started to swirl faster.

Ida caught her breath. Did this mean their mother was trying talk to them? She had to get Hanna and Magda! Running to the window, she shoved it open. Her sisters had just reached the garden and were making snow angels. "Magda! Hanna!" Ida shouted down.

They looked up as she beckoned excitedly.

"Come quickly! It's the snow globe—I think it might be Mother!"

Chapter Two

Hanna and Ida raced back upstairs and threw open the door. Then the three sisters gathered around the snow globe, each one trying to get as close as possible. Soft golden light was glowing brightly from the snow globe and the snowflakes whirled and danced at double speed.

"Mother?" Hanna said, giving the snow globe an impatient shake. "Are you there? Are you trying to talk to us?"

The girls held their breath
as an image of their
mother's face gradually
formed in the snowflakes.
It was wonderful to see her.
"My darling girls," she said
faintly. "Listen carefully, I do
not know how long I can talk for
and—"

"Where can we find the blue and purple
orbs, Mother?" interrupted Hanna.

"Hanna, shush!" said Ida.

Their mother's image flickered and started to
fade. "You must hurry!" she called desperately.
"Your aunt and I are locked in a fierce battle of
magic. She needs to stay close to me as she fights
to take my powers, but she will do everything
she can to try to stop you getting the remaining
orbs. She is using her powers to spy on you. You

have to reach the orbs before her! To find the blue orb, travel to where the crystal—" There was a noise like a howling wind. Her face disappeared and her voice faded.

"The crystal what?" Hanna demanded, grabbing the sides of the globe. "Mother, come back!"

"Mother?" Magda whispered.

There was no reply.

Ida bit her lip. "She's gone." Tears sprang to her eyes.

"And all we know is that we've got to go somewhere where something crystal is," said Magda in dismay, fighting back tears herself. "That's not enough of a clue."

Hanna pushed her hands through her hair. "There are so many crystal things. Even just in the castle."

"It must be something really special, though," said Ida thoughtfully. "The pink orb was in a snow hawk's nest—the only snow hawk with a silver tail in the whole of the island. I think we should go to the library and research what special crystal objects there are in Nordovia."

Hanna rolled her eyes. "You can look at boring books if you like but I'm going to start actually looking. There are lots of crystal vases and ornaments downstairs."

Pushing past Ida, she dashed out into the castle. Ida rushed off to the library.

Magda was left on her own. Oskar rubbed his head against her leg. "Oh, Oskar," she said, stroking him, "why do they always want to do different things?"

He made a contented whuffling noise as she scratched behind his ears, and then rolled over onto his back with his legs waggling in the air. She smiled. "Come on, then. Let's go and see if we can help." With Oskar trotting beside her, she went downstairs, thinking about her mother's words. Surely if they needed to look in the castle then their mother wouldn't have said they had to *travel* to the crystal object.

It sounded like they had to go on a journey. Maybe Ida was on the right track researching what special crystal objects existed on the island.

Reaching the hallway, she paused out of habit next to a huge tapestry of the Nordovian flag. It was the girls' favorite object in the whole castle, after the snow globe. Their mother had always said the tapestry was very special. It showed the three ancient symbols of Nordovia—the snow hawk, the full circle

of a rainbow, and the crystal rose . . .

Her heart turned a somersault.

The crystal rose! When they had found the pink orb it had been by a snow hawk's nest. Maybe the blue orb would be found where a crystal rose grew. . . .

She was suddenly completely and absolutely sure she was right.

"Oskar!" she gasped. "We've got to find the others!"

She started to hurry down the passageway that led toward the library. As she did so, she caught sight of Hanna. "Hanna! I think I've worked it out! We need to find Ida!"

Hanna questioned her all the way to the library, but Magda wouldn't tell her what her idea was until all three of them were together. They found Ida in a corner of the library and then, speaking in a whisper to avoid being overheard by Annika, the librarian, Magda explained her idea.

"A crystal rose," breathed Ida.

"That means the third orb could have something to do with a rainbow," said Magda. "The tapestry could contain all the clues we need!"

"You might be right, but we should focus on finding the blue orb for now," said Hanna. "So, where do crystal roses grow?"

"We're in the right place to find out!" said Ida. As she jumped to her feet, Annika came over. She was a tall thin lady who wore her gray hair in a coiled braid.

"Girls, do you need assistance?" she asked.

"Yes, please, Annika!" said Ida. "We need books about the flowers of Nordovia so we can find out about the crystal roses."

"Aha, a homework project for Madame Olga, no doubt," said Annika with a smile.

She hurried off, and a few minutes later she returned with a stack of books on the plants and flowers of Nordovia. "These should be of some use," she said.

"Thank you very much," said Magda politely.

They took the books and started to flick through them while Annika returned to her desk.

"Here. I've found something!" said Ida, pointing to a chapter on crystal roses. "Let's see what this says." Her eyes skimmed over the words. "Oh."

"What?" said Hanna.

"Crystal roses only grow in a single ice field in the foothills of the Hellsbaard Mountains."

"That's a long way away," said Magda. "Much too far to walk."

"So we take the ponies," said Hanna. The girls were confident riders and each had their own shaggy Nordovian pony in the castle stables.

"It says you have to cross the Great Glacier to get to the ice field. It's the largest glacier in the whole of Nordovia. The ponies won't be able to go onto it," Ida said. "It will be too icy for them—they'll slip and fall."

Hanna shrugged. "So, we ride them until we get to the glacier and then work out how to get across once we're there."

"Don't be silly. We have to have more of a plan than that," Ida said.

Hanna frowned. "Why?"

"Because it would be silly to go without a plan and—"

Magda hastily jumped in. "Listen, our first problem is Madame Olga. She'll never let us travel out into the mountains on our own. She barely even lets us go as far as the castle gates!"

Hanna's eyes glinted. "I guess the only thing

to do is to sneak out at night. Like we did when we went to find the pink orb."

"It makes sense," said Magda.

"Do you . . . do you think this adventure will be as dangerous?" Ida asked. It had been very frightening when they'd been attacked by the wolf.

Hanna lifted her chin. "I don't care if it is!"

Magda squeezed Ida's hand. "We'll all be together, Ida. Don't worry. We'll look after one another—just like we did before."

Chapter Three

The sisters hurried to the stables, making as little noise as possible. The sun had just set and stars were starting to appear in the sky. The stables were warm and smelled of sweet hay. The sturdy little ponies looked surprised to see the girls, but nuzzled them good-naturedly.

Ida had spent a bit of time that afternoon reading about the Hellsbaard Mountains, and had found a map that showed the shortest

route there. She knew the sharp ice picks she had drawn earlier would come in handy on their journey.

They attached them to the ponies' saddles along with the rest of their equipment and supplies. Hanna had sneaked into the kitchen when cook was having her tea break and taken some bread and cheese from the pantry for themselves, and some meat for Oskar, and Magda had found a bag of carrots for the ponies in their feed store.

Ida was carrying her sketchbook safely inside her coat. Everything she had read had made her realize how dangerous the mountains were. There were deep crevices hidden by thick snow, and a constant risk of avalanches—tumbling walls of snow that fell from the high peaks and buried everything in their path. She had an uneasy feeling that great danger lay ahead. Ida felt her skin prickle, wondering if their cruel aunt was using her powers to spy on them at that very moment. . . .

"Come on, boy," said Magda, leading Tommi, her pony, out of his stable.

Hanna was already mounted on her pony, Eira. "Hurry up! We've got to leave before the guard patrol comes past." Oskar gamboled around, eager to be off.

Trying to force her uneasiness away, Ida patted her pony Katla's thick mane and joined her sisters.

The castle gates were bolted, but Hanna used her magic and the bolts slid back easily.

"Here we go!" Hanna said in excitement. They urged their ponies on into a canter and then a gallop, heading toward the distant Hellsbaard Mountains that were silhouetted against the horizon.

Snow crystals flew up from the ponies' swift hooves, and icy wind stung the girls' cheeks. Oskar tried to race beside them but soon he fell behind. Magda glanced over her shoulder and saw him struggling to keep up. "Change size, Oskar!"

All Nordovian polar bears had the ability to change size. As a young cub Oskar got very tired if he changed too often, but he was going to *have* to grow now if he wanted to keep up with them and join the adventure!

Oskar shivered for a moment and then grew

as large as an adult bear. After that he had no trouble in racing along beside the ponies, his huge paws thudding down into the snow.

On they galloped. They rode through the outskirts of the dense forest, the place of their first adventure. The branches of the dark-green fir trees were laden with snow, and pointed icicles hung in shining clusters. After the forest they rode through the icy tundra, where the flat, frozen land stretched out all around. They kept heading toward the mountains that loomed in front of them.

It took them hours but at last they reached the foothills—the lower slopes where rocky shapes poked out through the snow. They had to let the ponies slow down to a walk so that they could pick their way around the boulders that littered the ground. The air was even colder there, so cold that when they spoke their breath froze into clouds of ice crystals.

"I'm glad we wore our warmest clothes," said Magda, pulling her coat collar up around her neck. "How much farther is it to the Great Glacier?"

"Not too far now." Ida had plotted their journey on a map and memorized it. "It's between those slopes over there." She pointed into the mountains. "The ice field where the crystal roses grow is on the other side."

They rode on until they saw the glittering glacier emerge from the dark sky in front of

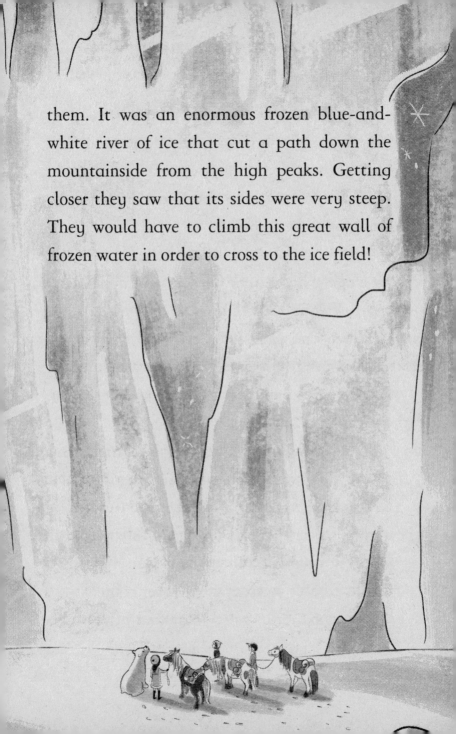

them. It was an enormous frozen blue-and-white river of ice that cut a path down the mountainside from the high peaks. Getting closer they saw that its sides were very steep. They would have to climb this great wall of frozen water in order to cross to the ice field!

"We'll have to leave the ponies here," said Magda, reaching down and hugging Tommi. "Thank you for bringing us this far," she told him. He snorted, and she had the feeling he was glad to be stopping.

The girls found a safe, sheltered spot—a cave at the base of one of the mountains with a small stream outside—where the ponies could lie down and rest. They removed the ponies' saddles before fastening on their stable blankets to keep them warm, and gave them the carrots they had brought.

The ponies had all been trained to remain where they were left, so there was no need to tether them. It would have been too dangerous to tie them up in case a hungry wolf pack chanced upon them. This way the ponies would be able to escape if danger came.

"Be good. Stay safe," Hanna whispered to

Eira. "Please be here when we get back." She
had no idea how they would return to the castle
if they didn't have the ponies.

Eira snorted and started munching her pile
of carrots.

The girls fastened their bags on their backs,
along with their ski poles and ice picks, and
headed to the glacier.

Ida stared up at the wall of ice in front of
her. She really didn't want to climb it but she
knew she had to.

Hanna inspected the ice. It wasn't smooth at
all, but scarred with large cracks. "I think this
will be the best place to climb," she said at last.
"There are good handholds and footholds. We
can also use our ice picks to help us if we need to."

"We'd better rope ourselves together in case
one of us slips," said Magda. "Hanna, you go
first, then Ida, and I'll go at the back."

Hanna tied the rope around their waists. She had to take off her gloves to fasten the knots. She gasped with the cold. "Brr!"

"Don't leave your gloves off for too long," warned Ida. "Your hands will freeze."

"All done!" Hanna said, once the rope was looped around their waists and secured. She fixed the last knot and put her gloves back on. "Are we ready to go?"

"Definitely!" said Magda.

"I guess," said Ida.

"Follow me as closely as you can," Hanna said. Her green eyes locked with Ida's identical ones. "You'll be all right," she added softly. "I promise."

Ida felt a little better, almost as if some of her sister's bravery had slipped into her, bolstering her courage. "Thanks," she said.

Hanna started to climb. She instinctively

seemed to find the best handholds and foot-holds, and when she couldn't find a handhold she drove her pick into the ice and used that to lever herself up. It was hard work. Gritting her teeth, Ida followed her and Magda climbed behind, encouraging Oskar.

The polar bear, still in his large size, used his long claws, digging them into the ice and haul-ing himself up the wall little by little. But it was hard for him. Polar bears were not built for climbing up steep slopes. Magda glanced back anxiously. He had stopped halfway up and was clinging to the ice. He had started to shake and tremble. "Oskar, come on!" she called, stopping to encourage him. "You can do it."

She felt the rope tug as Ida and Hanna kept on climbing. "Wait!" she called to them. "Oskar's in trouble!"

Her sisters paused just as one of Oskar's

back paws lost its grip on the ice. He scrabbled desperately with his free back paw and whimpered in alarm.

"Steady, boy," Magda said gently. She knew she had to try to calm him. If he started to panic, he would lose his grip completely. "It's all right. Dig your claws back in. Keep on climbing."

Her voice seemed soothe him. Fixing his eyes on her, he dug first one front paw and then the other more firmly into the ice, and then found a better grip for his back paws too. Bit by bit he edged up the ice toward her while she encouraged him on.

"Come on, Oskar!" Hanna and Ida urged. "You can do it!"

The polar bear reached Magda. Although he was large, he was still just a cub, and Magda saw the fear in his eyes. She stroked his soft fur. "Good boy," she said softly. "Let's climb together."

Slowly but steadily, she and Oskar climbed up toward the others.

Hanna reached the top of the glacier first and helped Ida over the edge, and together they helped Magda and Oskar.

"We made it!" Ida said in relief as they all sat panting at the top. Oskar lay next to them for a few moments getting his breath back.

"Well done, everyone!" said Hanna.

Magda nodded. She was very glad they

were all at the top of the glacier and safe.

Oskar nuzzled all three girls as if to say thank you, and they all gave the brave bear a huge hug.

"It's very empty up here," said Hanna, looking around the vast deserted expanse of ice and snow that glittered softly under the night sky.

"I thought it would be all smooth like a pond," said Magda. "But it isn't at all." It was rutted and bumpy, and covered with deep snow and patches of ice.

"Walking isn't going to be easy," said Ida, getting to her feet and taking a few experimental steps. She immediately fell. "Ow!"

"We'll have to use our ski poles," said Hanna, helping her up.

"It's going to take us ages to get across," said Ida, getting back to her feet. "We need to be really careful—all this snow could be covering crevices. They're like deep cracks. If we fall down one, we might never get out."

Oskar made a whuffling sound and lifted one front paw and then the other.

"What is it, boy?" Magda asked curiously.

He walked over and pushed his shoulder against her as if he wanted another hug. She frowned, sure he was trying to tell her something. Oskar nodded with his head across the glacier as if he wanted her to walk forward. With her hand on his back, she took a step or two. Her feet slipped but with her hand clutching his fur she didn't fall. Suddenly her eyes widened. "I think Oskar's trying to tell us he can help us! His paws are brilliant for walking over ice. We can hold on to him as we walk and he will help us balance!"

Oskar snorted as if in agreement.

The girls unroped themselves and then, leaving the rope on the glacier, they crowded around Oskar and buried their hands in his soft fur. It was much easier walking on the slippery ice with a big polar bear to hold on to! However, they still had to go very slowly. After half an hour their legs were aching from bracing themselves on the ice and they hardly seemed to have crossed much of the glacier at all. The far side still looked a long way away.

"This is really hard," said Ida, pausing to

take a breath beside a massive boulder the size of a cart. "It's going to take us forever to get to the ice field on the other side!"

Magda looked up at the snow-covered mountains towering around the glacier. "I wish we could just fly to the other side," she said.

"Well, *you* could," said Hanna, pointing to a

black-and-white bird with dark wing tips swoop-ing over the ice. "You could turn into a snow bunting."

"I'm not going to leave you," said Magda.

"No," said Ida quickly. "We should defi-nitely all stick together."

As she spoke there was a deep rumbling, thundering noise from high above them.

"What's that?" said Hanna.

Oskar cowered on the ice, covering his ears with his paws and shrinking to the size of a cub again.

"Oskar? What's wrong?" said Magda.

"Is it thunder? Is there a storm coming?" Hanna said.

"No, not a storm!" Fear gripped Ida as she pointed upward to where a deadly white wall of snow had started to fall from the mountain-tops above them. "It's . . . it's an avalanche!"

Chapter Four

The girls stared in horror as the wall of snow thundered down the mountainside straight toward them, tossing boulders into the air and sweeping up everything in its path as it gathered speed and strength.

"What should we do?" cried Magda.

A wind suddenly swirled, lifting the edges of their coats. "Nothing!" hissed a harsh voice. "There is nothing you can do! This is your time to die!"

"Veronika the Shadow Witch!" gasped Ida.

"Yes," their aunt's voice hissed through the wind. "I offered you a chance to give up on your quest to save the Lights but you didn't listen. This time I will not let you get the better of me. Goodbye, meddlesome nieces. Your journey ends here!" She gave a shrieking laugh that merged with the thundering of the wall of snow as it bore down on them.

The girls clung to one another. There was no way they could run and escape. The wall of snow was almost on them. It blotted out the sky, the moon, the stars—everything.

"We're going to be buried alive!" cried Ida in horror, staring up at the snow.

"No, we're not!" Hanna pointed to the massive boulder next to them. "Get behind that."

Ida opened her mouth to protest. "Just do it!" Hanna yelled, pushing her toward it. "I've got an idea!" Focusing on a nearby thick sheet of ice she used all her magic to lift it into the air.

Magda and Ida suddenly realized what Hanna's plan was and pulled Oskar down behind the boulder with them.

Frowning with concentration, Hanna used her magic to lift the thick sheet of ice above them like a roof.

"Stay down!" cried Magda as the thundering snow swept over the top of them, battering at the sheet of ice and the sides of the boulder. The noise was deafening. She and Ida huddled together, clinging to Oskar as Hanna focused on keeping the roof of ice over their heads, protecting them all from the snow and rocks and ice.

Magda could see Hanna start to shake with the effort of holding the ice there. "You can do it, Hanna," she urged her sister. "You can save us."

Hanna's mouth tightened. She could feel the magic sapping her energy . . . but there was no way she was going to give up!

Every second felt like an hour, but eventually the avalanche passed on, thundering over the glacier, sweeping up the deep snow on the surface and carrying it away.

As the noise gradually faded, Hanna lowered the sheet of ice to the ground beside them and collapsed. She was breathing as hard as if she'd just run a marathon and her face was pale.

Ida and Magda hugged her.

"Oh, Hanna, you were amazing!" said Ida.

"You saved us all!" said Magda.

Hanna smiled weakly. "I thought I wasn't going to be able to hold it."

"I can't believe Veronika did that," said Ida. "She really is evil!"

"She'd do anything to capture the Ever-changing Lights," said Magda with a shudder.

Oskar whuffled in agreement and nudged Magda with his nose. She gave him a small smile and stroked his head.

"You look exhausted too. Here, have something to eat," said Magda, hurriedly unpacking her bag. She pulled out the bread and cheese they had brought and gave some to her sister, then gave Oskar the strips of dried meat they had brought for him.

As Hanna ate, the color slowly returned to her cheeks. She sighed in relief. "That's better," she said. "You should have some too."

The sisters tucked into the bread and cheese. Food had never tasted so good. As they ate, the world settled around them and a peaceful silence fell once again.

Ida started to pack their things away, and Hanna tightened the laces on her snow boots. "We'd better get going," she said.

Her heart sinking at the thought of all the walking they still had to do, Magda stood up. She frowned in surprise. The avalanche had changed the glacier. Most of the snow had been swept away, revealing cracks and crevices in the frozen river beneath it. More surprising was that near to the boulder they were sheltering behind there was now a dark opening—a cave.

Going over, Magda saw that the cave led into a tunnel that ran down through the ice. Her heart beat faster. It seemed to head in the direction of the ice field. Maybe it led through the ice of the glacier all the way to the other side. If they could go through it, it would be much quicker than walking across the treacherous surface.

"Ida! Hanna! Look at this!"

Her sisters came out from behind the boulder. Magda showed them what she had found. "Do you think we could walk through it?"

"We should try!" said Hanna instantly.

"But we don't know where it goes," Ida pointed out. "We could end up wandering around under the glacier not going in the right direction—or we could be trapped by an ice fall. It's too dangerous."

"I don't mind it being dangerous. I'll go and explore," said Hanna, heading eagerly toward the entrance.

"No, wait!" said Magda, an idea springing into her head as she saw the same bird they had

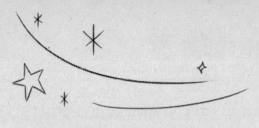

seen earlier flitting through the sky. "I've got a better idea. Why don't I turn into a snow bunting and fly through the tunnel?"

"It might still be dangerous even if you're a bird," said Ida uncertainly.

"I'll be fine," said Magda. "I can make sure it's safe."

She focused on the bird swooping down low over the ice and felt a tingle run through her arms and legs. *Wings*, she thought, remembering the feeling of flight from when she had turned into a snow hawk on their last adventure. Her whole body tingled and suddenly she realized she was soaring up into the air, wings beating. She was a snow bunting!

Joy rushed through her as she swooped in a large circle. She opened her beak and a whistling, warbling sound flooded out. She swooped into the tunnel. It was dim but not totally dark, the moonlight filtering down through the layers of compacted snow and ice. The tunnel twisted and turned, its blue and silver sides icy cold. The question was: Where did it come out? Magda spread her wings and flew on.

Hanna and Ida waited impatiently by the tunnel opening.

"I hope she's okay," Ida whispered.

Oskar whimpered and put his paws up on her knees. She scooped him up and cuddled him. He looked anxiously toward the tunnel too. He didn't like it when the girls were split up!

Hanna was the only one of them who didn't seem worried. "I wish I could be Magda right now," she said longingly. "Where do you think she is? Do you think she's reached the other side?"

"I don't know but I wish she'd come back," said Ida. *Come on, Magda*, she thought. She poked her head into the tunnel. "Magda!" she shouted. "Where are you?"

Only her voice echoed back to her. "*You . . . you . . . you . . .*"

"Let's not wait any longer. Let's go after

her," said Hanna eagerly. She hoisted her bag onto her back again and grabbed her ice pick. "Come on."

But just then they heard a warbling high-pitched whistle, and the next second a snow bunting came flying toward them through the tunnel.

"Magda!" Ida exclaimed.

The air shimmered and then their sister was standing beside them.

"Well?" Hanna demanded, looking at Magda's shining eyes.

"The tunnel *does* lead through the ice to the other side!" she exclaimed. "There's a snow field there with lots of glittering crystal roses." She grabbed her sisters' hands. "Come on! There's no time to waste!"

Chapter Five

"This is incredible!" breathed Ida as they made their way through the tunnel of ice. The tunnel's walls glowed and glittered turquoise, and above them was a shining roof of silver.

"It's like we're in a magical land," said Magda, stopping to touch the icy walls. The ice had molded itself into strange curves and swirls. The floor dipped down a slope. There

was a smooth patch of
ice running down one side like
a playground slide. Hanna couldn't resist: she
sat on her bottom and slid down it.

"Wheee!" she cried.

Oskar leaped after her. His feet went in all
directions and he ended up sliding down it on
his tummy. Magda and Ida giggled and followed on their bottoms.

"This is much better than trudging across

the surface!" said Hanna, jumping to her feet.

They hurried on. Around the next corner the tunnel opened into a huge cavern. Thick columns of ice—stalagmites and stalactites—stretched from the ceiling and floor. The girls gasped in wonder.

Hanna dashed behind a stalagmite "Can't catch me!"

Magda grinned and chased after her. "Bet I can!"

Oskar gamboled between them and tripped them both up. They laughed as they both slid over the ice.

"Come on, we'd better get a move on," said Ida. "We still have to find the crystal rose and the orb *and* get back before Madame Olga realizes we've gone!"

The thought made Magda and Hanna jump to their feet. They all ran as quickly as they could through the rest of the tunnel until they saw a hole with moonlight shining through it.

"That's the way out!" said Magda.

Hanna broke into a run. "Last one out is a rotten tomato!"

CRACK!

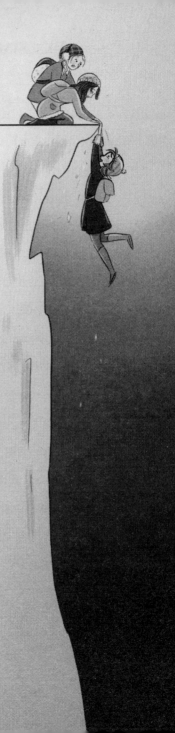

A wide crevice suddenly opened up right in front of her.

"Hanna!" shrieked Magda and Ida.

Hanna tried to stop but her feet skidded from under her and she tumbled over the edge of the crevice. As her sisters screamed she twisted around in midair, grabbed the edge, and hung on by the tips of her fingers.

Magda and Ida were beside her in an

instant. They threw themselves to the ground, and Magda grabbed Hanna's wrists.

"Hanna! Hold on!" Ida urged.

"I'll help you up!" Magda gasped. She leaned over the crevice to try to pull Hanna up. But Hanna lost her grip and slithered down the side of the ice. Her weight took Magda with her. For one heart-stopping moment Ida thought both her sisters were gone forever, but thankfully they landed on an icy ledge a few meters down.

"Are you all right?" Ida cried.

"Yes," said Hanna, glancing at Magda, who nodded. "Just a bit bruised. But how are we going to get back up to you?"

Ida looked around desperately. How could she help them? She needed a rope but they'd left theirs back on the surface of the glacier. Then Ida smiled. Of course! She could draw

one! Grabbing a shard of stone, she used the
pointed end to scratch a drawing of a rope
into the ice. She drew the rope looped around
a nearby rock and then drew more and more
coils of it. She swallowed nervously—she knew
she had to get this just
right. If it was too
thick, it would be
too heavy for her
to carry, and if it
was too thin, it
might not hold
the weight of
her sisters. Tak-
ing a deep breath
to steady herself, she
felt a familiar tingling run
through her body as she drew.

Finishing the drawing, she sat back on her

heels. The air shimmered, and suddenly a rope appeared just as she had drawn it. One end was tied securely around the pointed rock; the other was coiled up.

Ida whooped. She'd done it!

"Ida! What are you doing?" Hanna cried impatiently from the crevice.

"Trying to rescue you!" Ida shouted back. Grabbing the free end of the rope, she hurried to the edge of the ice. Her sisters were looking up.

"Here," Ida called, throwing the end of the rope over. "You can use this to pull yourselves up."

Hanna climbed up first, holding on to the rope as she scrambled up the icy sides. Ida held on tight to the other end of the rope to keep it steady as Hanna clambered over the edge of the crevice. "We need to help Magda!" she panted.

Together they helped Magda climb up. At

long last, all three of them were back on solid
ground. Oskar gamboled around them, rubbing his head against their legs.

"Thank you!" Magda said with a shiver,
looking back into the deep, wide crevice. "That
was really scary."

"How did the crevice open up as quickly as
that?" Hanna wondered.

"It must have been caused by the avalanche," said Ida.

"It's so wide. However can we get across it?"
said Magda, frowning.

Oskar grew to his full size and then galloped up to the crevice and leaped through the
air, landing safely on the other side. He turned
to them and chuffed as if to say, "I can do it!"
and then leaped back over, nuzzling each girl
in turn with his nose and looking pointedly at
the crevice.

"We can't jump like you can, Oskar!" Ida said, not knowing whether to laugh or cry.

Magda had her head on one side and was studying Oskar closely. "I think he's saying he'll carry us!" she said.

Oskar stood on his hind legs and made a happy whuffling noise before dropping to all fours again.

Magda smiled. "Well, here goes!"

She climbed on to Oskar's back and held on tightly to his soft fur. With a tremendous bound he cleared the crevice. Magda climbed off and Oskar jumped back over and repeated the leap, first with Hanna and then with Ida. The sisters gave Oskar a huge hug once they had made it over, and he shrank once more. They knew it took a lot of Oskar's energy to grow to full size, and they were very grateful that he'd managed to get them over the crevice!

"We did it! Ice field, here we come!" Hanna cried.

Moonlight shone through the round opening at the end of the tunnel. Holding hands, they ran toward it and burst into the open. A vast ice field filled with hundreds of glittering crystal roses was spread out before them. The roses grew out of the snow, and there seemed to be hundreds of them. A family of Arctic foxes, with large pointed ears, snowy-white fur, and coal-black eyes and noses, were playing between the flowers.

"It's so beautiful," breathed Ida, immediately wanting to draw the scene.

Hanna started to search for the orb, carefully pushing aside the translucent leaves of the flowers and checking around the plants. The ice field was massive, but the snow was so white and untouched she hoped it would be easy to spot a sparkling blue glass orb. However, as she began to make her way across the field, she paused. Something was happening! The ground was moving!

Dark vines and thorny brambles started to push up through the snow. They twisted around the crystal roses, spreading between the stems and covering the pristine snow. As they grew, the vines made horrible crackling noises, which sounded to the girls like mocking laughter.

"What's going on?" Hanna heard Ida say.

Swinging around, Hanna saw that the same thing was happening all over the ice field.

Ida tried to pull the brambles to one side. "Ow!" She gasped as the thorns stabbed her fingers, despite her thick gloves.

Magda's mouth tightened. "All these brambles must be Veronika's doing. She can't come here herself to stop us because she can't leave Mother's side for long, but she's using her magic to make it impossible for us to take the orb."

"What shall we do?" said Hanna.

The girls felt stunned. They'd come so far and overcome so many obstacles. Were they really going to be defeated now that they had finally reached the ice field? But how could they find the orb when there were so many thorny brambles?

"Okay, let's think about this," said Magda, her mind whirring. "Can any of us use our magic to help?"

"I don't think so," Hanna said.

Ida shook her head, there were just too many of the horrible vines.

Magda looked at the foxes now sniffing at the brambles and an idea suddenly came to her. "Maybe I could change into an Arctic fox and see if I can sniff it out? They've got really sensitive noses."

"Try it!" urged Hanna.

Magda focused on a nearby Arctic fox with a particularly fluffy coat. He looked at her with his sparkling dark eyes. As their gazes met she felt the tingling, and the next moment she had transformed into a fox just like him!

She spun around, yapping happily. She felt the urge to run and bound and smell . . . oh yes, definitely smell. The air and the ground were full of subtle scents she hadn't noticed when she was a human. There was the musky polar bear scent of Oskar, a sweet rose-scented smell that seemed to be Ida, and a scent of new grass and fresh air that was Hanna. She thought she could also smell a family of jack rabbits and . . . She breathed in deeply. Yes. Magic! She was sure she could smell magic. The scent was like nothing else, it made her nose feel tingly and sparkly. She looked at her sisters and whined, hoping they would guess she meant them to follow her, and then putting her muzzle to the ground she followed the trail. Luckily she could place her small fox paws between the brambles and thorns. She glanced back to see Ida, Hanna, and Oskar carefully treading a path between the brambles behind her.

The trail led across the field, the scent getting stronger and stronger until Magda reached a rose that was slightly taller than the others. Its flower was still a perfect bud, its petals tightly closed. *Here*, she thought instinctively. *The orb is somewhere here.*

Standing up on her back legs, she sniffed the flower. Yes, the smell was strongest by the bud. The orb must be inside its petals!

Hanna and Ida reached her.

"Where's the orb?" asked Hanna.

But Ida was looking at the way Magda was sniffing at the bud. "I think it's in the rose!" she said. "Is that right, Magda?"

Magda nodded and sat back, looking expectantly at her sisters.

Ida pulled off her gloves. "I'll try to take it out." When she touched the flower she gasped. "The petals are like ice!" She tried again but pulled her hands away, shaking her fingers. "Ow! I can't touch them. They're too cold."

"This must be part of the crystal roses' magic," said Hanna. "If we can't touch the petals, how can we get the orb out?"

Magda willed herself to turn human again. The tingling feeling whooshed through her body and she changed back into a girl. "Your magic, Hanna," she said quickly. "Could you use that to open the petals without touching them?"

"I can try!" Hanna said eagerly. Taking a deep breath, she drew on her magic and felt it welling up inside her.

Focusing on the rose, Hanna willed the petals to open. Magic surged through her, strong and powerful, and the petals slowly started to peel back one by one, the bud opening and blooming into a perfect translucent flower. The orb glittered in the center of it—a shining, sparkling ball of blue light.

The girls looked at one another, thrilled. "You've done it, Hanna," said Ida, tentatively reaching out toward the orb. She tensed as her fingers closed around it, waiting for the bite of ice on her skin, but all she felt was a soft, gentle warmth. She lifted the glowing orb and the blue light inside it swirled and twirled. It was absolutely beautiful.

Magda and Hanna hugged each other as Oskar chuffed in delight.

"We've got the orb at last! Now we can take it home and put it safely in the snow globe," said Ida happily.

Hanna bent and picked up a single crystal petal that had fallen when the rose had bloomed. It was so cold it made the tips of her fingers tingle. "I'm going to take this petal to remind us of our adventures." She undid her bag and put it safely inside.

"We'd better hurry home now," said Magda, glancing at the first traces of dawn creeping across the sky. "We have to get back before Madame Olga discovers we sneaked out of the castle."

"We should keep a lookout for Aunt Veronika's magic on the way," added Hanna. "We know she's been spying on us, so when she discovers we've found the orb she'll be really angry. She might use her magic to try to stop us."

The girls exchanged anxious looks. They now knew their aunt was ready to do anything to stop them.

Ida tucked the blue orb safely inside her coat. "Let's get home as quickly as we can!"

Chapter Six

The girls hurried back toward the tunnel with Hanna and Oskar leading the way. "Keep up!" Hanna urged her sisters.

"I can't!" Ida wanted to run fast, but her legs felt like they were filled with lead. She was tired after a night of riding and running and climbing and no sleep. "I really can't go any faster, Hanna."

"Me neither," said Magda. "In fact, I don't

think I can run much more." Magda flopped down on the ice, rubbing her aching legs. Using her magic to turn into the fox had completely exhausted her.

"You have to," cried Hanna.

Oskar bounded in front of them, blocking their way as he grew to his full size.

"What are you doing, boy?" asked Hanna.

Oskar looked around at his broad white back and made a sniffing sound. Then he flopped down.

"Whatever is he doing?" said Ida in surprise.

Oskar looked at his back again and then looked at the girls. "I think he wants us to ride on him," said Magda.

"Could he do that? Could he carry us all?" said Hanna. "He's never carried all three of us before!"

Oskar whuffled softly again and so they

carefully climbed on to his back—Hanna first, then Ida, then Magda. The polar bear stood up and they buried their hands in his soft white fur as he leaped forward. Ida gave a scared squeak. It felt very different from riding a horse. For a start, there was no saddle, and the polar bear bounded rather than cantered, throwing them up and down and side to side. Ida flung her arms around Hanna's waist and hung on tightly.

"Good boy, Oskar!" cried Magda as the polar bear raced into the tunnel. The crevice was still there. They squealed as he took a flying leap over it and sped onward! The blues and silvers blurred around the girls as Oskar carried them safely around the twists and turns of the tunnel and back to the surface. They emerged from the cave, and Oskar finally stopped at the edge of the glacier.

They all slid off his warm back and hugged him. "That was wonderful!" Hanna told him.

"Thank you so much, Oskar," said Ida, kissing his head. "I couldn't have walked much farther."

He nuzzled her and quickly shrank to his small size. He looked worn out.

"Look, the ponies are still there!" Magda said in delight, spotting the three ponies from her viewpoint on top of the glacier. "And our climbing ropes. Come on!"

Oskar was so small and looked so tired that Hanna put him into her bag with his head poking out of the top. He looked very sweet! Then the girls slipped and slid down the icy side of the glacier using the ropes to help them. It was much easier going down than it had been getting up! At the bottom they raced over to the ponies who were looking out of the cave. The girls greeted them with pats and kisses.

"Let's get the ponies saddled up," said Hanna.

Ida's muscles groaned at the thought of a long horseback ride. "I've got a better idea," she said. "Wait a moment." She took a shard of rock and scratched a simple sleigh into the ice. She remembered to draw a harness for the ponies and some warm blankets. She was so tired that it took a long time for the shimmering magical feeling to flow through her. But finally everything she had drawn appeared beside the ponies. The girls harnessed the ponies to the sleigh, tucked Oskar in, and made themselves comfortable. And then they were off.

"Yah!" cried Hanna, who was holding the reins. "Back to the castle!"

The ponies leaped forward in a flurry of snow crystals, pulling the sleigh easily through the newly fallen snow. While Hanna drove with a rug over her knees, Magda and Ida snuggled

down under the warm wool blankets with Oskar sleeping soundly between them.

As the sun started to rise in the sky, the sleigh swept across the flat Arctic tundra. The island was waking up—birds were starting to sing and red squirrels were scampering up tree trunks. A family of Arctic hares ran beside the sleigh for a while before falling back to tumble and play in the snow. The golden sky grew brighter and

brighter. But it was still only early in the morning. Maybe, just maybe, they would get back in time!

But as they entered the snowy pine forest, a bitter wind started to blow, making the trees' branches rattle and shake.

"What's happening?" said Ida uneasily. "That wind has come from nowhere."

Icicles fell from the branches overhead, plummeting toward the girls. The ponies whinnied in alarm as the wind gathered in intensity and ice crystals flew in all directions. The wind built to a shriek, and a familiar voice hissed through it. "You have not escaped from me!" The sound echoed around them, seeming to merge with the howling of the wind.

"Aunt Veronika!" gasped Ida, sitting up straight.

"We have to get out of these woods!" cried

Magda as more sharp icicles rained down from above, hitting their backs and heads.

"Come on! Let's go!" cried Hanna, slapping the reins to make the ponies move faster.

The ponies leaped forward, just as keen as the girls to get out of the woods. But as they did so, Ida squealed. Ahead of them, the trees' branches were sweeping downward to block their path.

The ponies forged ahead bravely, galloping on through the branches. Oskar woke up and whimpered in fear.

"We'll protect you, Oskar," cried Magda, reaching to pick him up. But she was too late. A branch was already sweeping through the air straight toward the little polar bear.

"No!" Ida screamed, and without a second's thought, she flung herself in front of the cub. The branch hit her full in the chest, knocking her half

over the side of the sleigh. For a moment, hang-
ing over the edge, all Ida was aware of was the
thundering of ponies' hooves and snowy ground
whizzing past just a few inches away from her
face. A tree trunk loomed ahead of her. She was
going to collide with it. . . .

She felt Magda grabbing her and hauling her up onto the blankets. The next moment, she felt Oskar licking her face and then Magda was helping her sit up. "Ida!" she gasped. "I thought you were going to die."

Hanna was looking over her shoulder from the driver's seat, her face pale. "Are you all right?"

Ida's heart was racing and she was short of breath. "Y-yes," she managed to stammer.

Oskar snuffled her face and climbed into her arms.

"That was so brave!" said Magda.

"Me? But I'm not brave," said Ida.

"Oh, you are, you really are!" said Magda, hugging her.

"Watch out, everyone!" yelled Hanna as another branch swept toward their heads. They all ducked just in time.

The ponies increased their speed and burst out of the forest onto the plains. As they galloped away from the trees the wind dropped. "We've got away!" said Magda.

The ponies raced on across the snowy ground. In the distance the girls could see the welcoming turrets of the castle.

"Gallop, boys, gallop!" Hanna urged, glancing back. She was sure she could hear the howl of wolves in the distance. Was Aunt Veronika sending wolves after them now? They had to get into the castle grounds as quickly as possible.

Come on, come on, she thought as the ponies thundered over the snow.

The castle gate was shut. There was no time to stop and open it by hand. Hanna drew on her magic. *Open!* she thought.

The gates flew open with a bang. The

ponies swept through and came to a stop by the stables. Their sides were heaving and their nostrils flaring.

While Hanna shut the gates and bolted them, Magda and Ida leaped off the sleigh and hugged the tired ponies.

"Thank you so much for getting us home," Magda murmured.

Working together, the girls unhitched the sleigh, put the ponies in the stables, and gave them water and hay. Then they let themselves into the castle through the servants' entrance.

"We made it," whispered Hanna in relief as they reached the main staircase. As she spoke the library door opened and Madame Olga emerged.

"Girls! Where *have* you been?" The sisters froze in front of their stern-looking governess. They were in so much trouble!

"Um . . . we . . . um . . . ," Magda floundered, hugging Oskar tight.

"We're . . . we're sorry!" Ida burst out.

"We really are," said Hanna.

"I should think so too!" Madame Olga sniffed. "Going outside at this time of the morning? Before you have even had your breakfast? This is really not the behavior I expect."

The triplets looked at each other. Madame Olga hadn't realized they had been out all night. She just thought they'd gotten up early and been out in the garden!

"So, what have you been doing?" Madame Olga demanded.

"We . . . we went out looking for flowers, Madame," said Hanna.

Ida and Magda exchanged a quick look. Well, they *had* been looking for crystal roses, although they couldn't tell Madame Olga that!

"Ah, I see, for your nature lesson this morning," said Madame Olga, her face clearing. The girls looked at her innocently. "Well, I am glad you were doing something useful and applying yourselves to your studies. Now please go and change your clothes!"

She swept away.

The girls' shoulders sagged with relief.

"I'd better draw us some flowers to take to our lesson later," whispered Ida.

Exchanging grins, they carried on up the stairs.

As soon as they were in their bedchamber they shut the wooden door and pulled off their boots. Hanna took the petal of the crystal rose she'd picked in the ice field out of her bag and held it up. It sparkled brightly in the early morning light.

"It's so beautiful," said Magda softly, thinking back over their adventure and everything they had seen and done that night.

"I never thought I'd see a real crystal rose," said Ida.

"Or that we'd walk under a glacier or survive an avalanche!" said Hanna. "It's been an incredible night."

"And all for this," said Ida, taking the blue orb carefully out of her coat. Looking at the iridescent light inside it, all three girls brimmed with happiness. They had had an amazing adventure and completed their task. The second orb was safely back at the castle.

Ida carried it over to the snow globe. As if sensing the presence of the orb, the globe began to glow, and the snow inside it began to swirl faster.

"Mother?" said Ida hopefully. "Can you hear us? We found the blue orb."

There was no reply but the globe shone even more brightly. Ida held the orb out to her sisters. They each put their hands on it and then slowly moved it toward the snow globe. The light grew brighter and brighter, then suddenly the orb vanished and the snow globe changed, flickering into beautiful swirls of pink and blue.

"The blue orb is safe," Hanna said happily. "We did it."

"You did, my dears." Their mother's voice echoed faintly around the room, making them all jump. "I don't have enough power left to appear in the globe, but I hope you can hear me."

"We can!" said Magda eagerly. "Oh, Mother, are you and Father all right?"

"I am growing weaker by the day." Freya's voice grew fainter. "And the more of my magic Veronika steals, the more powerful she becomes, and the more she finds out about the orbs. But if you can find the final purple orb by the Day of the Midnight Sun, there is still hope. Once you have all three, you will be able to free your father and me and help triumph over the Shadow Witch."

"We'll find it, Mother!" said Hanna.

"You must be quick," Freya said. "I am so proud of you, my darling girls. So very, very proud." Her voice was now so faint they could hardly hear it.

"Where is the purple orb, Mother?" asked Magda.

"To find it you will have to go on a dangerous journey through . . ." Freya's voice faltered. They heard her take a trembling breath. "The tapestry will help you," she said desperately. "You must . . ." Her voice faded and the light dimmed.

"Mother!" Hanna cried.

There was only silence.

"Oh no," Ida groaned.

"She's too weak to speak anymore," Magda said quietly. "And now we don't know where in Nordovia to find the purple orb."

"And the Shadow Witch might know more than us," said Hanna, remembering what their mother had said.

Hanna's eyes met her sisters'. "Wherever we have to go, and whatever we have to do, we'll find the orb before the Shadow Witch. We've got our magic powers to help us."

"And we've got one another," said Magda softly. "That's the most important thing."

"It is," said Ida, thinking back to the adventures they had just had.

They squeezed hands and looked at the snowflakes swirling and dancing in the beautiful pink and blue snow globe. They would rescue their parents and save Nordovia.

They had to!

The adventure continues in
THE FROZEN RAINBOW!

Looking for another great book?
Find it
IN THE MIDDLE.

Fun, fantastic books for kids
in the in-be**TWEEN** age.

IntheMiddleBooks.com

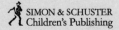

READ & LEARN

with *simon* kids

Keep your child reading, learning, and having fun with Simon Kids!

A one-stop shop where you can **find downloadable resources, watch interactive author videos, browse books by reading level, and more!**

Visit us at
SimonandSchusterPublishing.com/ReadandLearn/

And follow us @SimonKids

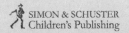
SIMON & SCHUSTER
Children's Publishing

The Unicorn's Secret

Read the books that started it all!

From Aladdin · Published by Simon & Schuster